בס"ד
לד' הארץ ומלואה

This book belongs to:

Please read it to me!

GLOSSARY

Abba – Father

Challah – Traditional Shabbos bread

Gefilte Fish – Ground fish, shaped and boiled

Ima – Mother

Kiddush – Special prayer recited over wine on Shabbos and festivals

Kugel – Baked side dish, similar to an English pudding

Mitzvah – Good deed, one of the 613 commandments

Shabbos – Sabbath

Shul – Synagogue

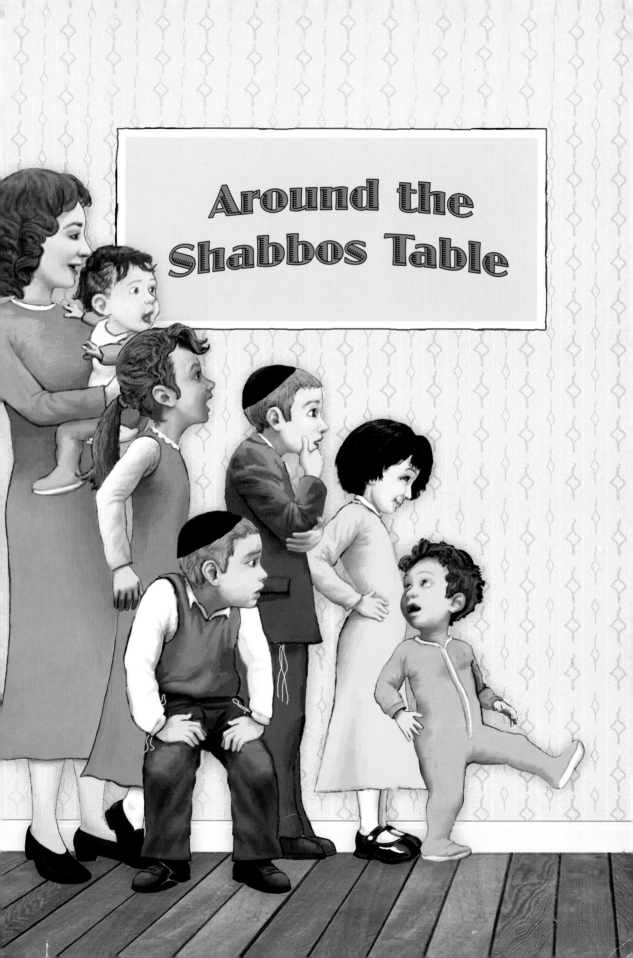

Around the
Shabbos Table

Around the Shabbos Table

For the best parents and in-laws around...
Rabbi Yisroel and Leah Gellerman
Rabbi Sidney and Raizel Berman. S.B.

• • •

In loving memory of my brother,
Rabbi Seth David Binus, z"l   A.B.

• • •

First Edition - 5769 / 2009
Copyright © 2009 by HACHAI PUBLISHING
Artwork © 2009 by Ari Binus
ALL RIGHTS RESERVED

Editor: D.L. Rosenfeld
Managing Editor: Yossi Leverton
Layout: Moshe Cohen

39910194   4/09
ISBN 13: 978-1-929628-44-5
ISBN 10: 1-929628-44-7
LCCN: 2008929416

HACHAI PUBLISHING
Brooklyn, New York
Tel: 718-633-0100 Fax: 718-633-0103
www.hachai.com info@hachai.com

Printed in Hong Kong

Around the Shabbos Table

by Seryl Berman

illustrated by Ari Binus

Hachai
PUBLISHING

Tova Leiba skipped to the door and flung it wide open.

"Hurray!" she cheered, "Abba is home from shul."

Everyone gathered around the table, faces shining, getting ready to begin…

...everyone but Yaakov.

"I'm tired of sitting on the chair near the wall," he said sadly. "People always bump into me when they squeeze by."

"Well," Eli explained, "I used to sit there when I was younger, so now it's your turn."

"I can't sit there," Sara said. "I have to be near the kitchen to help Ima serve."

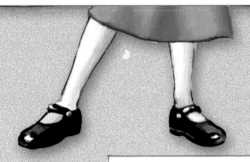

"Not me," announced little Bentzie, copying the others.

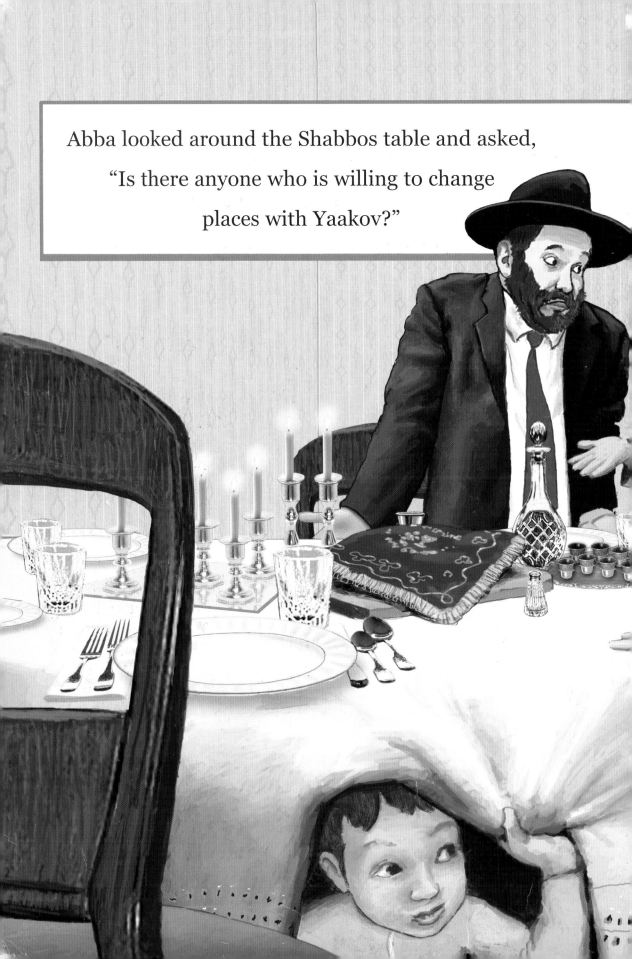

Abba looked around the Shabbos table and asked, "Is there anyone who is willing to change places with Yaakov?"

Tova Leiba thought for a moment and smiled.

"In any seat, no matter where, in any spot, in any chair,

Whether it is here or there, I'll be happy anywhere!"

And she slid over to Yaakov's seat.

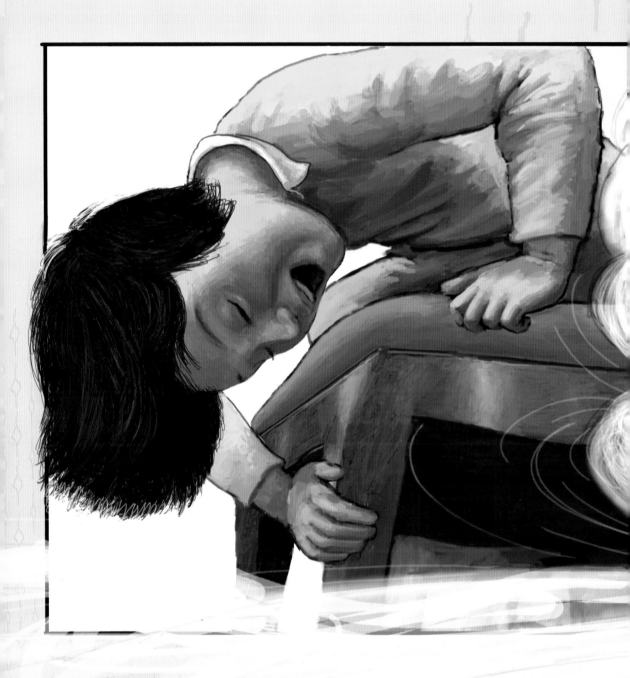

As Tova Leiba took a sip from the Kiddush cup, a gentle gust of cool air surprised her and tickled her ankles. "Where could that refreshing breeze be coming from?" she wondered.

Curiously, she peeked under her seat against the wall, and was delighted to find an air conditioning vent. Tova Leiba propped her feet right up against the cold metal. What a perfect place to sit on a hot summer night!

After everyone washed, Abba passed around the challah.
Everyone had eaten just a few bites, when Eli began
to wiggle in his seat.

"My chair is the worst. The stuffing is popping out, and it
sticks to the back of my leg. Tova Leiba's seat near the vent
is the best. I want to sit there."

Ima gave Tova Leiba a questioning look.

"Would you mind trading seats with Eli?" she asked.

Tova Leiba had been enjoying the air conditioning
so much. It felt great blowing on her feet, but she
nodded at her mother and replied:
"Here or there, in any chair,
I'll be happy anywhere!"

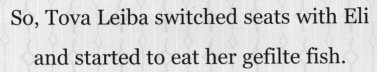

So, Tova Leiba switched seats with Eli
and started to eat her gefilte fish.

She didn't really mind that the chair had some stuffing popping out. Besides, this chair was right next to her father.

How Tova Leiba loved being near him! When Abba started to sing, he gently squeezed her hand and swung it back and forth.

Tova Leiba's heart soared, as she held her father's big strong hand, in the chair with the stuffing popping out.

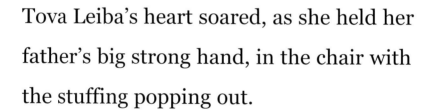

Everyone had just begun eating the soup,
when Sara jumped up.

"Oh, no!" she screeched, "I'm getting a chicken
soup shower! Look how the baby is splashing
me with her spoon! Why can't I sit near Abba
like Tova Leiba?"

Abba's eyes twinkled as he looked at Tova Leiba.
She smiled at her father and repeated:
"Here or there, in any chair, I'll be happy anywhere!"

So, Tova Leiba scooted over to the seat near the
baby while the chicken and kugel were served.
She didn't really mind sitting near her little sister.

It was so much fun to feed her!

Tova Leiba held up a small piece of chicken, twirled it around in a circle, and popped it into the baby's mouth. She took a little piece of kugel, bounced it up and down, and put it in, too!

The baby smiled and opened her mouth for more.

Little Bentzie watched the game. He climbed up near Tova Leiba to join in the fun. As Tova Leiba finished feeding the baby, Bentzie inched over, taking up more and more of Tova Leiba's chair.

Realizing how much Bentzie wanted her seat,

she whispered:

"Here or there, in any chair,

I'll be happy anywhere!"

So, Tova Leiba let Bentzie have her seat,

and she moved to his for dessert.

This chair wasn't

near the air conditioning,

or next to her father,

or even that close to the baby.

This chair, Tova Leiba

realized, was in the perfect

spot for her to enjoy...

...looking out of the window.

Tova Leiba could see the moon shining in the dark sky. She licked her ices and watched some people taking a Shabbos walk.

Naturally, she was the first to notice their neighbors, Mr. and Mrs. Bloom, heading toward the side steps.

"Ima," called Tova Leiba,
"We have guests for dessert."

Abba quickly opened
two folding stools.

Everyone was surprised.

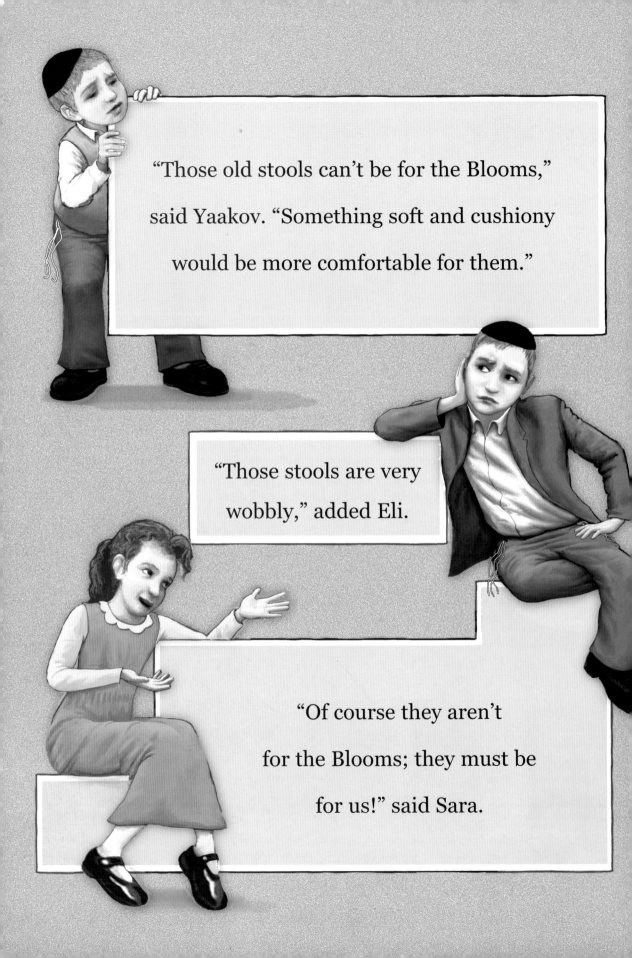

"Those old stools can't be for the Blooms," said Yaakov. "Something soft and cushiony would be more comfortable for them."

"Those stools are very wobbly," added Eli.

"Of course they aren't for the Blooms; they must be for us!" said Sara.

Tova Leiba reached for one stool and said,

"In any seat, no matter where

In any spot, in any chair

Whether it is here or there,

I'll be happy anywhere!"

Just then, Yaakov remembered
how Tova Leiba had found
something good about the
seat near the wall.

Eli thought about the way she enjoyed the chair with the stuffing popping out.

Sara pictured Tova Leiba having fun on the chair near the baby.

Maybe sitting on a stool wouldn't be that bad after all.

"I'll do it," said Yaakov suddenly.

"I'll give up my chair for one of the guests."

"Please, please, please," begged Eli.

"I really want the mitzvah."

"I think I should have the chance," Sara said.

"After all, I'm the oldest."

"Me, me!" said Bentzie, copying the others.

Tova Leiba's eyes lit up,

"I have a great idea," she said.

And what an idea it was!